AF674043

To The Moon & Back

Life, Love and Everything In-between

To The Moon & Back

Life, Love and Everything In-between

Poems by

Maria Goretti

Om Books International

First published in 2023 by

Om Books International

Corporate & Editorial Office
A-12, Sector 64, Noida 201 301
Uttar Pradesh, India
Phone: +91 120 477 4100
Email: editorial@ombooks.com
Website: www.ombooksinternational.com

Sales Office
107, Ansari Road, Darya Ganj
New Delhi 110 002, India
Phone: +91 11 4000 9000
Email: sales@ombooks.com
Website: www.ombooks.com

Illustrations by Sucharita S. Suri

ISBN: 978-93-52767-13-7

Printed in India

10 9 8 7 6 5 4 3 2 1

For my Zene & Zeke

May you always have abundant love and peace, to keep you warm
in mind, body, heart, soul and spirit. I love you both
to the moon and back many, many times.

Contents

Mad Love: Foreword 9
Introduction 13
1. Password Protected 15
2. Sparkle 18
3. For You 20
4. What If 22
5. Bleed 24
6. I Found a Me 26
7. Turbulence 29
8. The Last Time 31
9. Exactly 33
10. The Big Blue 35
11. Honeyed 38
12. Bare 40
13. Thank You 41
14. Your Heart, My Smile 43
15. A Chance 45
16. Scars Are Beautiful 47
17. Much More 50
18. This Is Me 52
19. Nothing Lost, Nothing Gained 54
20. Little Footsteps 57
21. Burn 59

22. A Speck of Sand 61
23. Unforgettable 63
24. Two 65
25. Star-crossed 67
26. Freedom Isn't Free 68
27. Mighty Rain 71
28. Chasing 73
29. Smudges 75
30. Friends or Lovers? 77
31. Find 79
32. Happy 80
33. Belong 82
34. I Do 84
35. War 86
36. Do You? 87
37. Optimistic 89
38. To the Moon and Back 92
39. Except You 94
40. The One 97

Mad Love

The book you are about to read is about many things. But they all intersect wonderfully with love. It pours out of the page. When I was done reading, I knew that she knew what love is.

If you ask me to describe what love is, I'd tell you it is poetry. If you ask me to describe what poetry is, I'd tell you it is love.

I'm an idiot, and that is exactly why I'm not capable of writing a book as beautiful as this one.

The written word is widely considered to be love's greatest enemy and yet … its biggest ally. So, when asked to write a foreword to a beautiful book, I hope to be an ally, not an enemy. As such, if this is bumming you out two paragraphs in, please do skip ahead at this point. The book gets so, so much better once you get to the poems.

I'm not even sure why Maria asked me, a comedian, to do this. Maybe it's one of those 'Hey mom, dad … I have been expelled' … 'What? How?' … 'Okay, not expelled … but I did wreck the car' situations.

Maria Goretti is your journey, I'm the dent in the side of your car.

All I know about love is this: The only real sign that you happen to be in it is that your behaviour immediately drifts towards the insane. It really is a spectacular form of insanity.

Love IS madness.

You start to see a person who isn't there in other people. You start to find meanings in the words of a song that could not be more clearly about something else. '*Watermelon Sugar*' is NOT about that one time you two went on a picnic. Concentration and any paperwork become damned near impossible, and yet you're able to agonise about every letter of a text message and its six thousand meanings. You immediately disregard that the other person might have other plans, and CANNOT fathom how they don't have the free time you do, to devote every second to them. You dress like you never do. You do things to your hair and face that make you look like someone you saw on TV … completely forgetting that *Rolling Stone* piece about how lonely they are. You tell lies about who you are, while hoping to hell they will 'see your truth'. You lose yourself in another person's body, you see yourself in their eyes, but you hate yourself in your own.

Love is pain, in both the chest and ass. It is a pain in the ass to find it, and we all know what a pain in the ass it can be while it sticks around. And yet nothing hurts more than when it leaves you, because it WILL not leave you, even after it's gone. That free fall to the bottom of your chest and the incredible climb back out of the darkness it bestows are where the greatest songs, movies, books, sonnets, and sugary carb-loaded snacks are born.

Love is freedom. It is the only time in your life when you truly get out of your way. It's like every cell in your body coming together to tell you to step aside. And when you do, albeit fleetingly, you're free. I'm totally aware of what I just typed, and NO, I am not on any drugs.

They say love finds you when you least expect it. I'm not sure who 'they' are, but I hope 'they' fall into a pile of something painful from a reasonable enough height. Just tall enough for gravity to turn into Karma for making stupid statements.

Stupid statements. That's the bottom line. Yes, love is chemical. Yes, love is biological. Yes, love is a feeling. Yes, love is energy. But more than anything else, it is a collection of stupid statements.

Love is words.

Ironically, it is both the perfect words, and the perfect 'loss for words'. It is waiting to hear the right ones, while speaking all the wrong ones. It is three select words to swear by, often interrupted by two VERY select swear words. It's ALL the words, and it's having NO words.

I have struggled all my life with finding these words. I'm pretty sure that's true for most of us.

So, when you read a book like this, where someone who CLEARLY knows what love is finds the perfect words, you know you are in the presence of something special. Words of madness, pain, freedom, longing, and loss. Words you feel like are ENTIRELY you. You were just never able to speak or write them...

What can I say? That's pretty poetic.

Enjoy this book, enjoy the road that is love, and apologies about the dent in the car.

Drive safe, Maria!

Vir Das

Introduction

So one September dawn in 2011
While my heart was smiling at heaven
A rhyme poured out line by line
And since then it seems, words and me were destined to be.

I write mostly about love, missing, distance, loss, memories, heartbreak and hope

That play a game with our intermingled lifelines, enveloped by beautiful forests, majestic mountains and deep seas that I feel always stay mine

These pieces from my book were meant to travel 'to the Moon and Back' many, many times.

So join me on this journey

I wish you lots of love, peace and healing for your lifetime.

I have poured my heart into these pages, and I hope you find bits that you would love to keep.

And please always know, what's meant for you will somehow make its way to you, even if the trek is steep.

Whether you let it stay or let it go away will be your truth
Much warmness,
And lotsa love,
From me to you!

Password Protected

You have always been sunshine through the storm
You have always smiled through a lot of inflicted, intentional
and non-intentional harm
You have taken life-altering tragedies within your fold
You have not let your energy get jaded
And polished your insides till it sparkled like gold

And yet you feel a missing…
So a part of you decided to find its own way
A part that decided to go with the flow
To trust in the now
Was it a good idea?
Only time will tell

In the meantime
Maybe your heart has been trekking through hell
And desperately trying to find ways to climb out
They say there is no way back, once you reach those depths

But this dark place is not for you!
You got here by mistake
You may have fallen in because you lost your way
You decided to walk with trust
That did not trust itself
And so it left to find its own path

And now you are standing just still
Among the warm ashes that still cling
to your once luminous skin
Looking up into the blue skies that are waiting for you
Swishing trees with butterflies in the breeze
Birds that sing
Puppies and kittens that roam free
You are the child of sunshine, stars and moonlight
Dark places are not for thee!

So look forward to all this new year has promised to bring!
Just let your charred bits heal

Let your soul rest
Wipe the soot off your face
Look at all the sun-shining faces beckoning you
And climb out of there
Pull yourself up with all your might
Your hair may still smell of smoke and burns
You are injured, but your aura still shines
Yes you are going to be fine
In a while

But for now
It's a tiny step at a time
There is so much you may want to do
With all the skill and immense talent, the one above has bestowed
on you
But first,
Go on, make sparkle this armour of thine

As for me
I'm not going to let anyone in, unless they really deserve me
This heart of mine is now 'password protected'
And I'm keeping it that way
Till I find my way to fields of sunshine I can call only mine
Till then, let's all keep practising being 'kind'.

Sparkle

There are broken parts in us all
That then eventually lose gravity
And cannot anymore fall
So they leap for the moon
And turn into stars
That, they say, peek out only when there is no light.
But, what are stars?
Do you know, anyway?
They are pieces that have come away from a burning mass
And taken off on an adventure through the Milky Way.
There are clusters
And then there are some that stand alone,
And you need no moon to see them shine,
In fact, the darker it gets, the brighter they glow
3/4 hydrogen 1/4 helium – that's what the learned say.
But I think, they are filled with
Dreams, wishes, hopes and desires,
All shining away,
They stay on a path,
Transcending your dreams, to a place,
On the other side
Half dark
Half light
And they no more put up a fight.
They have peace and smiles
All tucked inside.

So, every time you think
There is no other way
Hold yourself tight,
And watch that little ember in you sparkle away.

For you

I search for you in the little
things and in all of nature's
majesty,
I sometimes feel you will just
appear out of the blue.
Say hi the way we do
Put your arms around me tight
Push my hair away from my face

Kiss me like you never left.
And continue with conversations half kept
I search for you on timelines
And through the mayhem of cars going by
At airports among all the masked faces
And people that pass me by
I rumble through my dreams
Waiting for you
As you smile at me surrounded by flowers I love and trees
you keep
I search for you through my phone that never beeps
I search through all the words we exchanged
All the laughter that filled our sky
Through the lines on my palm that loved to rest on your heart
Through tangled fingers, coy smiles and sighs
I search for you at the edge of my lips and the drops that
fall from my eyes
I search for you in all that I do and all that I cannot
And in all this search,
I come back to 'me'
And, I stand silently
Trying to make peace with all that I am struggling to be
All the times I'm running away from trying to not
I am searching for that stillness, that peace
That love that lived inside me
I think it ran away with you
And that's why I'm searching for you
Because I'm searching for that 'me'
Who left one day to sit with you, wherever you may be
So, yes
I search for you
Do you search for me?

What If

What if the world was actually flat, instead of round
What if dogs barked, without a sound
What if seasons never changed
What if there was only laughter, and no pain
What if the skies never rained
What if grief was only momentary
What if kids never left and always stayed
What if the leaves never turned a fiery red
What if the sun never set?
What if you and I never met
What if you could take back all you last said
What if I never walked up your stairs
What if you and me built our own lair
What if you and me stuck to our own lines
What if we never shared that bottle of sparkling wine
What if we never sat under a sky full of stars
What if I'm from Venus and you are actually from Mars
What if we never shared our truths
What if we could not see each other
Under years of collected soot
What if we both had better timelines?

I'm searching for answers
Some, I know
And some I may never find
But today I was on a shooting set

Where my dialogues read, 'What if'
And, I was the one with all the answers
'Me' I had it all pat to the last line
But every time 'What if' left my lips
My heart just didn't stay mine
'What if' is something I have no answers to
If you do...
Can you help me?
Drop a line, or maybe three!

Bleed

This one here
Decided to walk one day
Without any fear,
Armed with lots of love and a heartful of hope

She flew straight into a song, she loved and knew
But a song is just a song
And it's anyone's to claim
And so the song flowed on without a care
In spite of loving it every day
She felt it leave her heart one day
But then it felt like it came back to stay
And she held it tight because she loved this tune anyway

She played it on loop
And took it with her everywhere
While she walked with a silly smile through her day
While she slept
While she travelled
You name it,
Everywhere!

And then one day
It did not play anymore
And, though she hummed the tune
The lyrics disappeared

Then the rhythm and bass
She was left with sounds that felt like heartbreak
She picked up the pieces
And buried them with all the rest of the memories that lay bare
And spent time, watering it with tears, she shed

Give it time, someone said
Give me time, she said
And in a bit there were flowers blooming
All over this soggy piece of earth
She looked at all the flowers
They reminded her of her love
They looked just like –
But she could no longer utter this name
That's the promise she made
So she gathered the flowers, and kissed them softly
Breathed their scent
Held them tight
And she let her heart, silently bleed into the night.

I Found a Me

I found a me
From long, long ago,
When I looked at her
She looked contrary,
Maybe, she was on an eternal quest
Searching, waiting, hoping

I tell her,
You will be fine
Your fears will dissipate
You will walk tall
And fall in love
With someone who awakens you
From a deep slumber
Someone who heals you
And stays like a song
Or possesses a soul that shines

And sometimes, they could all be rolled into one
But, fall in love you will
With man, woman, child, animals, mountains, forests, plains and deep oceans
With all the magic, this universe holds within.
You will make mistakes and fall
You will get up
Wipe the tears off your face

And bravely walk on...
You will meet infinite souls
And traverse different planes
Till you know
Love resides deep in you
But stop, you must not
Because to travel is your rest
Your destination of Zen

You will have children
Whom you will fiercely love,
You will stumble over boulders and pebbles small
Your heart may be broken
And broken many times by the ones you invited in
Maybe, they are not to blame,
Your soul was not their home
And every time this happens,
Rest assured
You will discover a piece of you
Sparkling even brighter
Reformed and new.

And that's what I see today
I see eyes that have loved
Lost and loved some more...
The rest, in my opinion
Does not matter anymore

I have learnt
I don't have to hit back at a wrong
Karma serves us all,
It gives us what we dole out

It always pats us gently
On our most vulnerable spot
So I tell her
Nothing in this world matters
Except how much and how well you love...

And so I look at myself and say
Continue to love
Even through trials and tribulations, stand strong
Keep your heart childlike,
Try not to expect anything in return
It's going to be difficult
But love nonetheless,
Till it sears and burns...

Turbulence

And there you were
And there was I,
And it mattered not
How we suddenly met
What mattered is what you said—
When your eyes met mine,
Something transpired
Something shook the core of our being
Made us stop and wonder,
Something we already knew
Something familiar, slightly changed
What were we till then?

We lived with a knowing
That something was unearthing
And yet
It felt serene,
Turbulence felt sane,
There was comfort
In balancing on a tightrope, blindfolded.
And then, life happened
We began to question routine
Love is one and many things
Who said love is peace?
Peace is acceptance
Love is turbulence

Love sets off the Richter scale,
To a degree of nonconformity
You cannot measure it,
Nor can you explain it
We never ever need to define love
It just is
Wrapped around us
In the brown of your eyes,
In the silence of your laugh,
In the softness of your mouth
Unhurriedly searing my lips.

I have your name tattooed on my breath
We don't need to shout from unseen rooftops,
We don't even have to whisper,
We just have to be,
Our usual, the same
Turbulence, you and me.

The Last Time

The last time I held you
It felt like the beginning of spring
When we kissed
It felt like the universe knew this was beautifully true
When we said bye
It actually meant, see you soon

It's ironic how our lives met
At a crossroad
Where parking or stopping was not permitted
And yet we did

Now that's fate, don't you think?
Yup, fate!
With heartbreak written all over it, in a big bold neon sign
That we decided to ignore.

So, when I see you again
Will the signal turn red, amber or green?
That's in the future, so curiously unseen
But I can't take anymore heartache
I'm still trying to piece 'me' back together
So, I'm avoiding all the roads
I'm walking only on tiny paths, untrodden
I'm not going to build anymore picket fences with everything
unsaid
So, while I go about my day
I pray, that in peace and love
I will find my own way.

Exactly

If you want, we can watch the moon together
You and me
You, from your point of view, me from mine
We have always been chasing full moons
You and I!

But reality is a long journey
So I'm going to just thank my stars for you
And one day when this distance between us
Is just skin,
And you can see that trusting you was my biggest thing,
Looking into your eyes, I will ask you
Do you still believe that I will be the bearer of your pain?
When all we both do is time-travel
To smear each other's faces with kisses and smiles
But yes, heartache is what we have gained
You will always stay a part of my life, you say
But not too close
Because you will hurt me one day,
How do you know?
I want to scream
But then you disappear,
And my smile follows you like a wild mare

Yes, I have very few things to share
I'm not perfect

But who is anyway?
I know one thing,
We will search for this love everywhere,
If I find you again, my heart will burst in stars
But...
Today I'm settling for the full moon,
I know you are sitting in her glow too
Wondering if I miss you?
Well, if you want to know the truth?
That's exactly what I do.

The Big Blue

When your heart is smiling from shore to shore,
Wondering how deep it dived to connect with your soul
Spinning to the depths of an inviting deep neon blue,
And, nervous as hell
I found my calm
Sitting in a shell
Lost but happy, roaming free,
Echoing, swim along with me

I finned my way through the blue
This was my me time, my perfect muse,

Filled with starfish, clownfish, sea anemones, eagle rays and sharks too…
And every time I surfaced, I knew
This turbulence,
Would help me find my truth.

If you want to reach deep into anyone's soul,
You must go beyond the surface you behold
You must be able to take that risk
You have to trust,
What may exist?
You need to respect
What's on the other side?
Because that's where true love resides

And, I met him under the roaring waves,
Under all that laughter
And madness,
I found that calm
And I knew this could do no harm
It was gentle, kind, loving and warm,
With a streak of madness that moved so strong.

Love is funny,
And arrives unannounced
It surprises you like a jack in the box
Pounces on you when you least expect it to
And really frightens your insides out.
But then, isn't that what love is all about?

So, I looked into his naughty eyes,
And smiled
I let him do what he does best

Make a complete clown of himself…
I listened to him as we followed each other around,
But, if he wanted me, it had to be an equal tide
Where we didn't have to hold each other too tight
And yet, we wouldn't ever let go, but swim alongside
I feel like a mermaid
But not half complete,
This is the beginning of a new me.
I'm happy I'm able to feel this deep
The scars of life have been washed away by the tide
And I am okay not to be wanting to take sides.

Love, I know, is never a decision one has to make,
And, yet, I have decided to walk with love
No matter where it decides to trek.

So, I am leaving you
With everything I have not said
And hope you can fill in the gaps
And meet me on that mountain up ahead
Where we can sit under the stars,
In the arms of our favourite tree
And look at the waxing moon
Playing hide-and-seek
And if truth be told,
No matter how much I love you
I want you to be you
And me
To just be me …

Honeyed

I let my guard down
I fell without caution
I walked into your arms
With music, flowers, freshly baked bread
All buttery, soft and full of passion
Never was there more sync
Then when your heart dived into mine
Magic!

That's what happened
I could always feel your soul
Even when far apart
Nothing else mattered
I felt as brave as a lioness
Walking freely through her jungle
I was crossing the river
The stars were witness
So was the moon
But that path to you
Disappeared, only too soon
So I stand by the water's edge
And wait for a familiar tune

The tree that we marked as ours
I sit there through seasons
I guess you did not trust
Or think I was brave enough
Whatever it was
You changed my lifeline
With wild flower honeyed memories
That canoe to meet the moon
And as I walk along the eucalyptus grove
Forget-me-nots graze along my ankles
Reminding me
Of all I am
And all I will be
Thank you for awakening me
Maybe that's why we met
You and me.

Bare

Naked thoughts
Bare face
Words dancing in a frenzied race
Life has taught me that time lets you pace
Demons that you can dance with
At an arm's distance with enough space
Moments
Battle scars concealed in a smile
And a tight embrace
Optimism – that's the name of the game
Just know, the sun will rise again
But you know right
Sunsets teach you
Goodbyes are stunningly beautiful too!
And deep down, you know what's right for you.

Thank You

Just want to say, *Thank you*
Ever since we crossed paths,
Little bits of joy just walked into my heart
And one day quite by chance
My insides knew,
That my heart belonged to you!
Was it the air?
The breeze, the soft swishing of the leaves
Or the way you said my name
Maybe, it was your eyes
They looked at me in a certain way.
Half man, half boy
We may not be perfect for each other,
I am all twists and road blocks
Just like unbending you
But something in my heart,
Tells me to hang on
We will be more than averagely okay
I know the universe will set it all right
I know we will have days filled with enough sunshine
And nights spangled in starlight
And the shadows, we make friends with them on our way.

I'm not the easiest person; you will slowly learn
Will you love me less if I'm out of turn?
I'm full of fear

And yet I'm bold enough to open my heart to you,
I'm stubborn, I don't give up easily,
I'm short tempered and fuse readily
I think I'm mostly right, which is wrong
I love too much or not at all
I don't have balance or practicality
I'm mercurial and unpredictable
I cry uncontrollably
I hope you learn to love the bits of me that are not nice at all.
And so,
If you are okay with us not being like everyone else
I'm here
I'm in this with you
I love you and will be true to you
I know I may have said this before
But just indulge me, today
If you think you can handle me,
Just stay
I think our love will find a way.

Your Heart, My Smile

In the deepest corner of my soul
Sits a girl,
Wondering about her smile
You may ask, why?
Well, she gave it away
To someone who touched her heart one day
And, it never returned
It has been a while.

She looks like a stranger to herself
Knows not what to comprehend,
Life is walking past, steady and slow
She saw him pass by
The thief of her smile
But, she realised she was naïve to think
Someone would give her back
What she so freely gave away?
She learnt this the hard way.

So, I led her on a long path
Unwillingly, she strode
With an armour around her heart,

I could not make her stay
She needed to find her own way.
As the dark night blanketed the sky
And stars lit up like dancing fireflies
I felt peace and knew she was fine,
A little lost,
A little confused,
A feeling of being slightly obtuse.

Before I fall asleep
I just want to say
Keep my smile
It's perfectly okay
Maybe, with you
It was always meant to run away.

But
I'm wearing your smile
The one smeared on my face
The day you kissed me
The one that said you missed me
The one that did not stop
When you heard me laugh
The one you sent in a glass of wine
The one you sang to me for a while.

So, give your smile away
If someone needs it today
And know, you will always have a heart full of smiles,
Pouring your way.

A Chance

And then she opened up her heart,
Inhaled deep
And as she did,
It connected her to a world
Flooded with myriad colours of fluttering gossamer wings
That only the woods would keep,
She dived in with all her might
Swam through the deepest blues
To reach the sunniest earths
She came upon this mighty tree
And watched in awe how the sun bid farewell to it
Every evening, so beautifully,
With hues of gold tinged with splashes of red
It was like there was so much more to love
So much to yet be lived and said
She loved sunsets
So, she followed the path that seemed to lead
To where the sun could be asleep
She loved how he stretched out his arms, held her close
Looked at her through his lashes that held gold
While she kissed his nose.

What she did not bargain for
Was not finding him anywhere
He had moved a few latitudes away

And while searching for him, she lost her way
Now, she is walking through a land
That just has moonless nights, no days
She picked a light in the sky to guide her way
But since she did not know, one from the other
She is sitting a bit askew
Enveloped in a cobalt sheath
Trying to call out to shooting stars that travel through
She is trying to find her way
She is different today
Since she let her insides free
A little brave
A little, let's see where life leads me
She has decided
She will love like it was meant to be
And as she continues her search, she whispers,
Just take a chance on me.

Scars Are Beautiful

Scars are beautiful
Don't ask me why?
They make you want to caress them
Though they may not feel all fine
Somewhere deep within,
Some scars stay for a while
And others are etched
Forever, they shall remain.

Visible scars are difficult to hide
But, what about the scars deep inside?
How do you heal them?
Do they ever go away?
Or, do they stay
As reminders of what you loved and lived by?
Do they hurt when you beckon your heart?
Or, do they make your soul melt
When you whisper a name?
Does it ache when you hear a familiar tune?
Or, look at a path that, may not be, home again?

What about the scars
That no one can see?

And no one will ever know
Unless they are willing to drown,
Deep inside your soul
What do you do?
With the scars
Residing beneath layers, armours and walls?
Well, join the dots…
Make a little map
That weaves a story
Of how a lamb transformed into a lioness
Have you ever looked into a lioness' eyes?
Pools of pure liquid gold
And, if you can your stare hold
You will see
She is as soft as a lamb,
Nursing the same fears as you and me
She wants to keep her loved ones safe
And provide all that she can
To guard the little ones
With whom she runs and hunts.

I sometimes hear her purr with joy
Sometimes, hear a cry in her voice,
I listen to her roar, see her play with her cubs
Prancing in the lair nearby
Sometimes, she runs after her kill
Fury ablaze like a forest-fire
She sits sometimes and just stares
And lets out a cry into the wild skies
Sometimes, licking her wounds after a fight
She limps away softly whimpering,
Broken by life…

Not every battle is meant to be won
Just like some hearts,
And so, what we are left with, sometimes
Are only scars
Big, small, deep
Some, only skimming the surface
Keepers of stories and memories
You may or may not want to recall
Love your scars, own them,
They are the truest stories of us all.

Much More

To put it simply,
I can't love you any less!

Much more is the only way I know
But how can I knock on your door?
When you don't live there anymore.
You walked away
Stopped saying, "I love you" one day at a time,
And then you disentangled your fingers from mine.

Do you remember?
Come away with me, you said.

Let me tell you how I feel without any expectations?
I walked into your arms,
Like a homing pigeon to her nest.
I believed you!
I trusted, what you said you felt,
Let this not be a forgotten chapter in my life, you said.

And now, I'm left to deal with the forgetting,
And all the chapters that are staring at me from the aisle,
Watching, your heart walking away from mine,
You mean a lot to me, let me show you, you said.

And now, the show is over,
The music has stopped playing

The flowers are all lying strewn
A shooting star waves bye

The skies all dark,
And the full moon looks at me
And she begins to ask me, why?
Your love healed me in more ways than you know, you said!
But who is going to heal me?
Did this thought ever cross your mind while you led your heart,
Seamlessly across into another timeline?

Soul on a journey the wise ones say
Love, apologise, forgive
And walk peacefully away

I have nothing more to ask of you or even say
Not a squeak
Just an ocean full of love that is for keeps

So thank you!
For tearing my heart open
Maybe, this will help me find,
What I have been searching for in this lifetime.

This Is Me

This is me
You say, when you send me pretty flowers
That spend with me a day
I'm flattered
But,
How would you know?
You don't really know my soul
We have just probably crossed words and swords
That spelt out magic in the air
Our worlds were never meant to meet
Just collide
And what was unsaid rose up thick like dark clouds
Only to pour down like rain
And be washed into the sea
There was no reservoir for stolen moments
No dam to hold them safe
So, the sea became my friend
And I turned to my heartbeat again
And slowly found you

I realised you were many things
Not just the waves that I adored
You were the whirring sand
Breeze and mountain peaks
The grass, I love to lie on
Sand that kept me warm, when I squinted at the moon

You were, sometimes, my calm and at times my storm
Sometimes, my silence and often my song
There are days when all I want to do is
Stop you, from you
And kiss your worries away
Wipe that crease between your brows
Untangle your knots
And send them into space
I love you
That's the only unsaid line
And yet you left me
One teardrop at a time,
As you flowed
And I wiped my face
I knew there will always be more of you
Deep inside me
That will surface

So, I let you be
I let you live inside me
And when you leave
I will not cry
Because, if there were no 'hellos'
There are no goodbyes.

Nothing Lost, Nothing Gained

Alone we came into this world
Alone we will go
I know the drill
I need no one to tell me so…
But, the time I spend on this earth
I don't want it measured by seconds or years
I want it to be a life I love
With the ones I hold dear.
I want it lived
With varied moments,
That will have my name etched
Tattooed on my soul
Forever more…

It does not really matter
If this moment we spent,
Is all we may have
Sometimes, I want everything
And otherwise crave that second of nano proportions
Is that too much to ask?
There is just us
And nothing else in this moment

So, should I just stop?
And let this pass
Pretend
We do not exist…

I give up
My tears are spent
My love, I leave for you,
Till the worlds end
It's lying on a boat
Somewhere mid-sea
But if you are frightened of the waves
Just let it be.
I'm going to walk back
To the place I know,
Sit among my flowers
Amid a weather that's growing cold.

This love I have
Is flowing no matter what,
It's a part of me
And that's how it will be.
I guess, you will never understand

How it feels to hold my hand,
To look into my eyes
And escape from this world…
To gaze deep inside my soul,
To hold me closer than my skin
Yes, I may be a wee bit too much
Too overwhelming to touch
Too much to behold,

If only you could speak to my soul.
But maybe, it's better this way,
Nothing lost, nothing gained.

Little Footsteps

Sometimes, I look back,
To a time when my footsteps were little
And I ran with my soul free
I never ever thought much of it
And how happiness and joy filled my being
All I thought about were exam papers, the next day
And the self-ironed pleats on my uniform so grey
I prayed that it would rain
So I could make paper boats
And watch them float away
On some boats, I wrote letters
On others, I drew
I did not know much
I loved the rain, I knew.

Sometimes I see that little girl in me
The one who made paper boats
Free
Happy
Innocent
And full of dreams
I meet her now and then
She has that big broad smile
I remember so well.
Sometimes we talk
Sometimes we just smile

Sometimes I ask her
If this was what she thought life is like

She looked at me today
You are fine, she said
You have forgiveness in your heart
And can love like no one else
You are overcautious
Oftentimes, so carefree
And, sometimes, as quiet as the deep sea.
Tears well up
When I sometimes look into my eyes
And quickly, I put on my smile
I'm going to stay happy
I'm going to stay blessed
Because, as I sleep peacefully at night
I know, I have a little angel with shiny wings
Sitting right next to my bed,
So, good night and God bless.

For my sister Juliet,
I love you and miss you.

Burn

All the running through the fields
All the climbing on mulberry trees
All the summers laden with ice creams
All the sandcastles and summer breeze
All the golas we slurped with glee
All the mangoes we robbed freely
All the butterflies we chased
All the snails that left their trace
Tom and Jerry that we watched on end
How we drove our mom around the bend
All the muffins that never made it past a day
All the crazy amount of prayers every day,
All the frilly dresses and spray set hair
That my dad gifted us and made us share
All the sea shells and warm waters we loved
All the chickens that my grandma shoved
Into the coop before the end of the day
All the sunny sides my uncle whipped up
All the chocolate, we licked
Inviting the ants to bed
Reading under blankets
Getting our dolls in our garden, married
All the brawls
All the garden prowls
Our tree house on the drumstick tree, that was not for keeps
Listening to the Beatles sing in the afternoon breeze

Childhood was really wonderful
Even though the September Garden meant
Buying canes for our bad deeds
And then it all ended one day
And our hearts cried out May Day, May Day
We all grew up overnight
And did not even put up a fight
Innocence flew out of every door
But waited around, till we could grow no more
And then returned silently, to hold us all tight
We held on to what was left on our insides
And tightly bottled up, our cries
Walk on, walk tall
That's the only way to be
When your life becomes an open-to-all country
You learn to live in between the pointed fingers,
And self-taught blame
You learn to stay still when the wind howls around you again
It takes long, very very long
And you may never heal
But you look back in time
And all you were
And go back to the ones, you laughed, fought with and cried
The one you denied
And then there were just two,
The youngest one took his staff and went to tend to the sheep
And carried along all your years of pain
But left with a 'missing' of all, and more
So when I look back, to 'today'
I will always remember
The day, my childhood burned.

A Speck of Sand

There is no life without a tussle
No understanding without being misunderstood
No heart without longing
No love without an eternal wait.

And yet, this life is beautiful
In all its brokenness,
Misunderstandings and tumultuous escapades,
And in the wait for what will never be ours.
In this wave that cannot be caught,
The water kisses the farthest sands
The grain of sand washes itself clean
Of the past and sparkles like never before.
Does it wonder about the next wave
That may or may not reach the shore?

I'm not half as brave as that grain of sand
I'm only human
Flawed and incomplete
Exactly like I was ordained to be.
And then comes along a wave
That engulfs my being

And though it feels like
I'm losing myself, being displaced
That there is no terra firma
And I'm being tossed around...
A part of me loves the sea
And all that it holds,
Its beauty and brooding ways,
And a part of me is disquiet
About its unpredictability
Its menacing tide and intensity
Life never gives us a choice,
Like tides don't allow waves to just be
They are sent hurtling to the shore
Whether they want to or not
Did anyone ask the sea
If it wants to be quiet and laze around
Or, get into a fury?
Everything is preordained
You can't choose to be the sand or the wave
Like you cannot choose whom to love
You just have to give in
To the tides of life...
Sometimes you come out a pearl
Or just a speck of sand whirled around.

But you must know,
This is not the end
You are in the right place,
It's just that your time to shimmer and shine
Is right around the bend.

Unforgettable

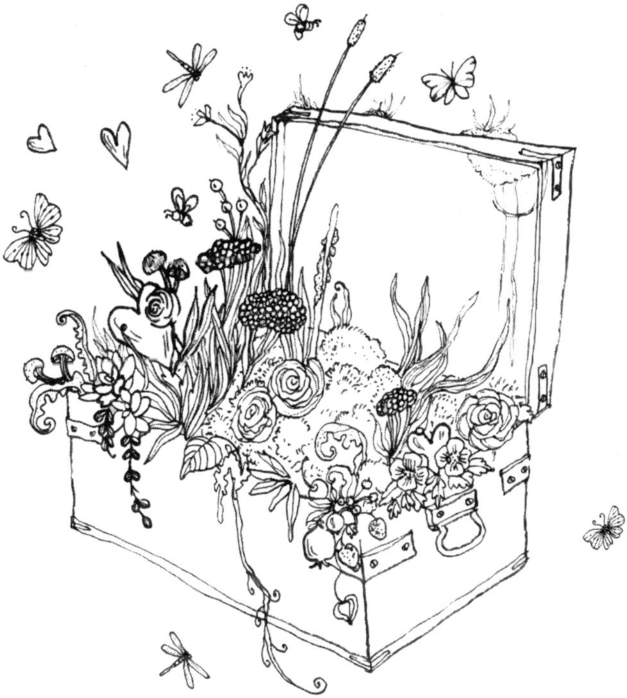

There has to be a place
Where I can take my broken pieces to
A place that knows how to thread it all together with loving glue,
A place that does not ask me how or why,
Where I smile a lot
And have no more tears to cry

Where the shadows stay away,
And my truant mind is not at play
Where glistening dewdrops lead my every pathway
Where I'm caressed by butterfly wings,
And wake up to birds singing a new sonnet every day
A place where the deer and the squirrel sit calmly in the grass,
And wild cats prance a bit away.
A place, where shooting stars know my name,
And smiles surround my heart like a strong dependable frame,
Where the mighty pachyderm silently walks his pace,
My heart feels at home in this place

I think I'm going there
Just me and my thoughts
All bare!
I have nothing more to lose
I'm just carrying all my pieces anyway,
It's going to be rearranged by the magic of the moon.
And when I find my way out again,
I will be differently beautiful,
That's what the forest whispers to me, every day
So come, walk with me
I'm lost
Hold my hand tight
We have a long way
And let me tell you,
It's going to be addictively unforgettable, every inch of the way.

Two

Somewhere under a crimson sky
While the sun is setting the world ablaze
I sit, waiting near the water's edge,
Wondering
About my life
Which is a maze
I get lost
I get found
I laugh uncontrollably
And sometimes cry without a sound,
I walk in my own company
With all my thoughts walking ahead
Reminding me of people and places
I may or may not wish to forget.
I look at the setting sun
It lures me to its crimson edge
I run into the sea and scream,
Wait for me,
Waves surround me in a rush
Confusing me with their musical embrace
Some pull me in, others push me away.
There are many to love
And yet we are in search of that one
The one who makes you feel
Like you have never felt
The one who tears your heart open

With his silent strength
The one who creates magic without casting a spell
Who caresses your soul
Reaches out to you, with the rays of the morn
And with moonbeams when the day is done,
Who talks to you, through the words of your favourite song
Who whispers your name
Like it was the most delicate sound,
Who runs his fingers through your hair
And kisses you like you are what the bees don't want to share,
Who knows when your laugh is real
And when your chatter
Is just all you may have to disguise your fear,
Who listens to your silence
Knows your laugh lines
And tears too.
Who makes you feel like a woman and a girl
Who wants your beautiful body as much as your scarred soul
Who can reach you through a crowded room with his smile
Who waits for you to finish, while you talk a mile
Who sends you rainbows on a rainy day
And snowflakes as summer dawns.
I could go on and on
But Morpheus has caught my eyes
Oh, yes...
There is so much in this world to love
But sometimes, just sometimes,
It's only about two people
Us.

Star-crossed

Loving you,
Is the simplest,
Yet most mixed-up my heart has felt.
What I think we share
Is not just a chemical reaction
Or molecules colliding,
Nor is it just the biology of touch,
Distance and time are just not fractions
Maybe somewhere we wished for a heart like us,
And the stars responded with you and me,
Star-crossed, they decided, it should be
And I know some days you feel cobalt
I feel that shade too
But when I close my eyes and stand on my toes
To kiss your lips,
And feel your arms wind around the small of my back
I know this path though not the smoothest will be on track,
And so I'm going to continue to love you
In the only way I know,
Truly and completely!
And I know you walk this path too.

Freedom Isn't Free

Freedom
That's what fills my soul
It's a bit scary
But it brazenly rips through my bones.
So, is freedom really free
As it is made out to be?
I meet him often, you know
He is as beautiful as I had imagined
He makes me laugh
With stories from lands I have not travelled.
I want to elope with him
Even if for a moment
Just to feel what I think he feels
To chase the wind
To dive into waters deep
To lie down under a starlit sky
And laugh till there are just sighs.
So, we walked along
And talked too much
He held my hand
And smiled
He looked at me in a way that burned my soul

Tore down my defences
Till my heart had turned molten, like liquid gold,
Our eyes communicated in ways
We never did understand
It was like Tony Bennett in concert,
Just for us, in the grand stand
I felt his arms wrap around me
His lips on a teasing trail,
Soft and full of love.
I looked into his eyes
As he held my face
And I realised, freedom is not free
He never let anyone into his heart
That was his part
And so, he was not free to love me.
The open roads he could travel,
Wound around him like Medusa's curls
And I saw freedom
For the first time...
Burn
He was not free
And scared about what he could feel
But, I was free, and living in the now
Because I could love him
With all my heart...
I let him walk
I saw him leave
He had his own little demons
With whom he had to deal.
He kissed me goodbye
I felt love oozing out of every pore of me
I felt free.

My love, my darling freedom, I whispered tenderly
Allow yourself to feel so deep
That it transforms your soul
Not just words, but for real.

Mighty Rain

I went for a walk today
While dark clouds rose up in the sky
I wished to be lost in the howling winds and rain
I wanted to shut my ears to the words
I wouldn't hear again
And listen to my heartbeat, instead,
I walked among the crowds, all alone,
While tears drenched my soul.
I wanted to yell out to the winds
And ask for an armour, to wrap around my heart
That is not as strong or smart,
Dried leaves and flowers pave the way
As I run
And chase the tears away.
Why do I feel so?
I have asked myself before
This feeling of isolation
It's a trick my mind plays with my heart
And makes me feel I'm miles apart
From whom I love and who I am.
I look up into the myriad shades of grey and blue
I'm going to let thunder strike
At the heart of me,
And when I'm done,
You will see a light
Whose embers burn,

A fire in my soul
That always takes me home,
Keeps my heart intact
Despite all the faults and cracks,
Pays off my debts to the universe
If I have not, yet
Run free
My heart says to me
But I'm rooted like a banyan tree.
So I sit in the pouring rain
As thunder calls out my name.
Well, I'm not going to lie
I just want to cry
I have a dam of thoughts
But now, the walls are coming apart
Bursting at the seams
With all my feelings and dreams.
It's my day to sit in the rain
So, let the dark sky dance in all its glory
I want to be free of everything
Crush the walls I have around myself,
Break them with all my strength,
I'm letting myself go,
Abandoning common sense.
I'm walking in the mighty rain
Because I know
At the end of it all,
I have nothing to lose,
Just all my pent-up pain.

Chasing

Chasing full moons
You and I
And yet we are always a few days short of its luminance
Whenever we try
We caught it unknowingly, one night
Unaware of what it had in store for us then
So, was it the brilliance of the moon
That shone in our eyes?
Or, was there softness already lurking there?
Whatever that was
I think we both knew
Something was different about the way you looked at me
And I looked at you.
And since then, all we do is chase the full moon
That's eluding us, like it does not care
Like it enjoys our pangs of despair
Like it does not know what it did to us
When in all its glory it shone.
And so we sit together in the thick of trees deep
Gazing at a sky full of stars
With no full moon up there
And I think, we love it better that way
Just the brilliance of our souls, shining away
And our laughter echoing through the night air
And so much love
That it makes the cobalt night jealously stare

Is this not enough?
Do we still need to chase the full moon
For an approval that what we have is actually beautiful?
If you really ask me, I think, I'm beginning to no longer care
I'm happy with a sky full of stars
And conversations, I find in your smile
The ones that start at the edge of your lips
And take over my heart
The one that jumps at me
From your loving eyes with that naughty spark
The one that knows the names of all nature and its art
The one that looks straight into my eyes and melts my insides
The one I know is filled with a love that no one often finds
The one that starts with a kiss and goes on for a mile
The one that starts with a game of blocks
And ends with arms around me tight.
Do we really need a full moon?
No!
Not me
Not when I can stare into the softness of your brown eyes
They seem enough
And yet, I know
You need to figure
Will a sky full of stars that sometimes shoot do
Or, is there a full moon somewhere waiting for you?

Smudges

And at the end
Smudges on paper
That's all that's left.
Can't read the words anymore
They are smudged
I am not the one I once was
But to me,
You will always be the one who changed me.
Distance does not really matter
In the vast ocean of my happiness
Photographs over time
Still make a pretty picture
Don't we know each other so well,
That we don't know each other at all?
Familiar words
And smiles,
Hysterical laughs
And sulks
Waves on an ocean shore
Pick yours,
If you can.
I'm just going to stand
At the water's edge,
Let each wave touch me
And with each nudge of its embrace,
I inch away from the ocean's vastness

I sit down on the sandy shore
And stare at the setting sun,
I know that it must go
Giving way to the brilliance of the moon
Yes, nothing lasts forever
Neither the warmth of the sun
Nor the magic of the moon.
Smudges on paper
Illegible words
Smiling eyes in the album of my heart
And when I sleep at night,
I look and search
For the smile that lights up my eyes,
And I know that at the end
Smudges on paper
That's all that's left.

Friends or Lovers?

Hey, stranger
You look at me like we could be more than just friends
I don't know if this could lead to walks into a forest deep
Where we both sit near a rambling brook
Wondering
Should we or shouldn't we take the plunge?
And so we meander
Speaking of all we have in our heart and head
Like we need to confess our lives
With no judgement and no lies
We look at each other
Unlikely ties
And yet there's something
Probably two souls searching for answers
We did not find.
Life often brings to you
Whom you may need at a particular time
Some for solace, some with a glass full of wine
Some as a bridge to another life
Some to open your heart and let you exhale!
Sighs and smiles that may have been stored,
Just so they could me mine
Do we belong to each other or to one's self?
Don't tell me,
Just answer this yourself.
But does your heart beat faster

When you look into my eyes?
Do you break into a smile when you say my name?
Do you have butterflies you keep
That come fluttering out, each time we meet?
Does your skin sparkle when our hands touch?
So what is this
Is this love
Or, just a phase?
I don't understand love anymore
It's far more complex than simple folklore
It's not all made up of only happy rhymes
And it changes its face through our lifetime.
So, I let us be
It feels comfortable, like it was meant to be this way
I like this path
It's not all pretty with flowers strewn
It's muddy, filled with pebbles,
Wild flowers and trees that are strangers to me
Sounds that soothe and yet are a bit scary
But we continue to walk at our pace
Talking about our lives and how we have lived this race
Till we reach the river's edge.
So, should we walk through
Because there's so much left unsaid?
Friends or lovers
Do we have to pick sides?
Or, can we be both, for each other in this lifetime?

Find

Today I need a holiday from my thoughts
That constantly find their way to you
I again dreamt of you
You were starting a new life
How did I know
I saw that big happy smile on your face
And my insides died
I packed up the little pieces of self-respect, I had strewn on your bed
Said farewell to the tigers, who walked peacefully away from me
They could smell fear no more
I realised I had to finally leave
I had to go find that girl
That girl who believed in love, rainbows and happily ever afters
Sunshine and optimistic twinkling stars
I had to find her
I had to find the love-filled, fearless, beaming, sun shining me.

Happy

Happy thoughts, dark thoughts
Flower side by side
That's the way life unfolds
But I'm going to look at the happy
That is my kind of gold
All the love, laughter, tight hugs, kisses, misses, and more
I'm weaving them into a blanket of the softest kind
That will cover me from the tip of my nose to my toes
And snuggled in it
All my love I will keep
Warm and away from the misery of dark thoughts and the cold
This that I have woven, is big enough for you and me
It's magical you know
Because every time I'm snuggled inside it
I can feel you next to me
And so I just close my eyes
And put my arms around you like I do,
Caress your scars, kiss the tip of your nose that I love so much
The curl of your lash
The warmth of your mouth
Your fingers that run patterns on my skin
All this and more
Laughter, conversations and the sound of pretty birds
Whose names I will never probably know
I love to ask you questions
Just to hear you speak

About your dreams and your fears that you keep
And then all of a sudden, I can't find you anymore
I think you have walked into the deepest part of a forest
Where you think it will all be safe
But I know the places you go to hide
I too have hidden there multiple times
So that no pain could find to me a path.
And then one day, as I sat on a tree
My heart just looked at you and knew, no more hiding for me
I'm going to live and love
And take chances like I must
What's the worst that could happen?
I will fall to pieces
Okay, but this time
I will put them back differently, with a lot more love
Because that's all I have inside
Kintsugi, that's the only way
And so now, I have you and my blanket of memories
So, good morning, my beautiful day
Look after me today
I'm going with happy thoughts, come what may.

Belong

I love being yours
Do we belong together?
Because we are torn by what it is
And what it could be?
Whom do I belong to I sometimes wonder
When I don't even belong to me?
I belong to shooting stars and beautiful songs,
To old oaks that I hold up since their limbs are no longer
   that strong
I belong to my laughter and the fears that live in the
   depths of my soul,
I belong to the azure above and wild paths below,
And yet I'm yours
Are you mine?
Can you hold me without it all being perfect and fine?
Can I rest in your heart?
Can you wrap me in your arms, that make me feel safe and calm?
Can I hold you tight, as I wake up to a new dawn?
Let me know
Because I seem to be walking a tightrope every day
I'm forever scaling half-dome peak
With no sign of you anywhere
I'm tired
I want to stretch my legs,
And breathe a sigh of butterfly wings,

And just lie down on a bed of grass with ladybugs and
other little things.
Your fingers entangled in mine,
Where we can watch clouds go by,
And make new plans.
I'm heading to the top of that mountain
I can only see the peak
I'm not sure of what the road is like;
But if you are passionate about sharing this unforgettable
journey with me,
Hold my hand
Walk with me.

I Do

If you think I miss you,
Please!
That's totally untrue.
In fact, missing you is not what I do
I do emptiness, longing and heartbreak
With tears that have a spring in the deepest part of me
And feelings that make me want to run to thee
But missing?
I don't want to commit to just that word.
My heart just hollers,
And there is no one to answer
I look at the moon that we both so love,
Are you watching her as she glows and broods?
Are you trying to reach deep inside me?
Well, I have left
I'm sitting on the grass near your favourite tree
Waiting with laughter, chatter and bubbly,
I have sent a message to the pachyderm clan,
And the shooting stars too,
They are all waiting for you.
I walk to that path you said was just ours
The one that has our kisses all over strewn,
The one that connects us to the world on the outer,
The world that keeps our reality
I wonder when you cross that path
Do you think of me?

That's our place
You and me,
And I know, one day
We will sit there in peace,
And reminisce about the times
When you could not be you and I could not be me.
But I think the shooting stars have carried my wishes up above,
To the one who makes the grand plans
And if this path is long and windy
And you decide to go another way,
Just send me a message through the birds you know,
Tell them my name,
Tell them I'm not afraid of the truth
But tell me,
So that I can stop searching for you along the way
Till then, my love,
I'm staying yours.
And will keep on loving you like I do
Madly, crazily and happily
As for missing you?
I don't know what that means, do you?

War

When we went to war,
with our hearts and our heads
With warfare set,
Strategies planned,
And emotional treaties negotiated
You chose to battle for you,
I chose your side, too!
Who chose me?
I never thought of this before
But today I ask myself,
Who is on my side?
Not you,
Not even me
I was at war with no armour
Just a heartful of hope and a battlefield ahead.

Do You?

I remember you in crazy laughter
In the songs that I keep for after
In the stupid jokes
In long conversations about your life
How we ate chocolate in tiny mouth-melting bites
In coffee, when I wake up late
In small morsels of everything, mixed on your plate
I remember you in sips of water, in the middle of the night
Blue skies that turned dark with all its might
Puffy clouds that passed us by
That squirrel that had a particular time, to fly
In tumbling blocks of jenga, if you please
In the afternoon breeze
In butterfly wings
In bugs that bite
Animals that roam free
Big beautiful trees
At the end of flights
In cuddles in the middle of the night
In the warmth of your breath
How you looked at me with so much love, in the soft of your eyes
How you made my skin melt
Your fingers entangled in mine
Many glasses of wine
Bubbles of champagne
Shooting star nights
Your eyes immersed in the brown of mine
I remember you in early morning kisses

And late night chats
Tightest of hugs
In the nothingness of prolonged silence
A goodbye
I remember
Do you?

Optimistic

*A*nd then sometimes...
Bam
In the middle of a beautiful day
While I'm deeply involved with a movie on TV
She looks into his eyes and holds his face
And you just hack through the bramble I built, and barge
back inside me
Can you please stay on your side of the road
I have not strayed off mine
And yet my heart finds its way to you like a drunk,
Who surprisingly knows her way, all the time
I breathe slowly
Really slowly
And look at my hands
And how they fit into yours
How much we smiled
Our world, though small
Was filled with everything the earth could provide
Grains of satiated dew drenched mud
Lofty trees agreeing with us
Chattering birds pushing us to hatch plans,
Wandering animals from the promised land
And fireflies that flickered in our eyes
We were filled with stars even during the day
Chatter, laughter and plans
That were never to bear fruit
What idiots, you and I
Too good to be true

Did you pinch yourself often, too
Some stories are too beautiful, they say
Because someone wrote them up in their own artistic way
How two hearts met one day
They probably were never supposed to cross ways
And yet, their world collided
And it seemed like it was all going to stay
You may say that's being too optimistic
But maybe
I like to always keep it that way
The moon though was brewing different plans
It tossed them up and down,
Like it sometimes does to the waves in a bewitched sea
Maybe that's why, the most beautiful love stories you only find on 'TV'
Reality has a different story to play
Each character is not given any lines
Just situations you navigate through and a tightrope to balance on
Sometimes you walk through beautiful flower-filled meadows
And sometimes arid land
There may be no setting sun or rising moon like the movies too
Your days are sometimes filled with moments
That you may not find in the story you pen down
Before you close your eyes.

Love is a bit whimsical and difficult that way
But keep the beautiful bits in your heart
And one day
It will find its way!

To the Moon and back

And so they travelled miles,
Just to hold each other tight.
For all they had was paucity of time,
She would always break his heart, he said.
No, not completely true, she said.
She would be breaking two, she knew,
One his,
One hers
But then he said goodbye
And broke her heart into fragments of a different kind,
Because at that moment, she could not make it right,
And he did not have the time
They both deserved a heart that could be home
She looked at all the love she held that only had his name,
To the moon and back, several times.
She scattered it all around him
Hoping the clouds, the flowers, a few paths, butterfly wings,
Babbling brooks, wandering wild animals, chirping birds.
And the breeze that caressed his skin,
Would always remind him

Somewhere, in all the chaos and din
A girl who had not stepped over lines,
Jumped over walls and broke through life's barricades,
Just because she loved him.
But she has all the odds stacked against her,
And time was never their ally
Was this not meant to be?
Is this how this story ends?
Well, I don't know
A little courage and a lot of hope,
Make dreams come true, they say.
But right now
He and she are travelling miles to the moon
And back again,
Only in opposite ways.

Except You

Not everything works out in life the way you imagine it to
Not the love, not the friendship, that fabulous job or that perfect travel plan
And in that moment when it's all lying in pieces at your feet
And you are reading every meaning about Kinstugi
When you are knocking on various types of helpful doors
When you feel like death
With no interest in anything
Least of all yourself
And digging deeper into an abyss, desperately trying to find that part of you that you miss

At that point of time
I have realised
That it's better to give in
Than to give yourself false hope

"This is for the best,"
You mostly lie to yourself

There is bigger and better waiting around the bend
And no I'm not going to disagree
But your heart needs to feel a little pain-free

You are unique and your healing has its own timeline
Don't be hard on yourself

Dive into the darkness of no answers
And slowly after going through every scenario and
conversation in your mind
With many ifs and buts rearing their concerned heads
You will come to a place where all you want to do
Is never get out of bed

Frankly
"I have realised no one needs you
Except you."
Read this a couple of times slowly to yourself

Because if you look around
You see life going on
The ones who want to leave have left
The job now belongs to someone else
You may no longer have that friend you held
And that holiday sailed on time with a bagful of smiles

What you will be left with is you
So be kind and loving to thee
Maybe you are not where you wanted to be
And as much as you may not like it
You are just going to have to give in to the universe's plea

Do a free fall into you
Trust what your gut is telling you
Don't wait for what tomorrow may or may not bring
Wrap yourself in that blanket of love
Take your time, I know it may seem like a lifetime

But when your heart is better healed
You will find yourself sparkling like freshly washed porcelain
Lingering scent of wildflowers, delicate and completely
not-breakable-free

But ready for freshly brewed tea

Somehow today
I just want to say
Hang in there
We are all in different stages of repair
Both you and me.

The One

A relationship they say is like a dance
It takes two to tango
One to lead, and one to follow
Let me share with you my thesis
And feel free to not agree with me
But I would like to differ.

Because sometimes
It actually takes just one
That really special someone
Who stands still in the storm
The one who does not fall
Who does not leave
Even though they may have the key
The one who does not give up through disharmony
The one that makes it work
Who smiles through all the hurt
The one who waits, for the storm to pass away
And dusts the debris like it were hay
The one that waits for you to find your way home
And always keeps everything warm
Tells you that this too shall pass
With just the kindest heart
Talks to you about growing old together
And with you is willing to face all kinds of weather
The one who is the strong anchor many feet below

While the boat on the surface is facing a raging storm
Most of the times it's about a soul
Standing in the wings
Waiting for the curtain call.

When the applause stops
And the make-up is off
And the audience have all gone away
If you have that person
Smiling at you, like you are all the stars in the sky
And, holds your hand as you walk and talk away
You have the 'One'
The one, who does not want to get away.

While you walk through life,
This role gets reversed, innumerable times
But as long as even one of you believes in 'we'
You have a chance
A chance to rework your magic, till eternity.

Acknowledgements

This book has really been long in the making…Mostly, because I was unsure of sharing my thoughts and words...But there are a few souls who helped me take that leap of faith.

And so...

Thank you so much Ipshita Mitra for your time, sound expertise and assistance in dissecting my words and bringing this collection of poems to fruition.

A big thank you for your artistic interpretation Sucharita S. Suri, my words feel so beautiful with your artwork.

A special 'Thank you' to my friends Jaya Misra, Sambo Parakh, Mini Mathur, Radhika Sawhney and Rick Roy who have read each poem of mine, encouraged me to keep writing, gave me constructive feedback and funny reality-checks.

And then there is the stranger I went trekking with and by the time we came down the hill, we were friends—Ajay Mago thank you for always standing by me and trusting me, it means a lot…